5/14

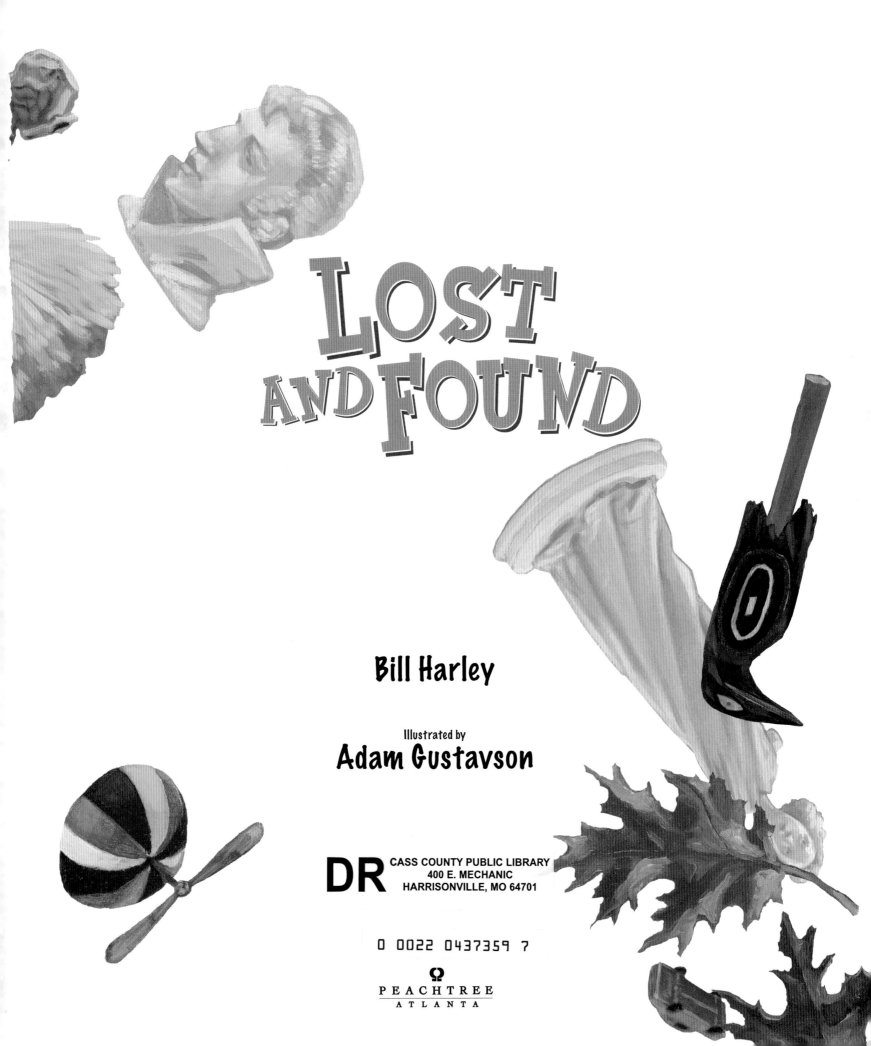

LOST AND FOUND

Bill Harley

Illustrated by
Adam Gustavson

PEACHTREE
ATLANTA

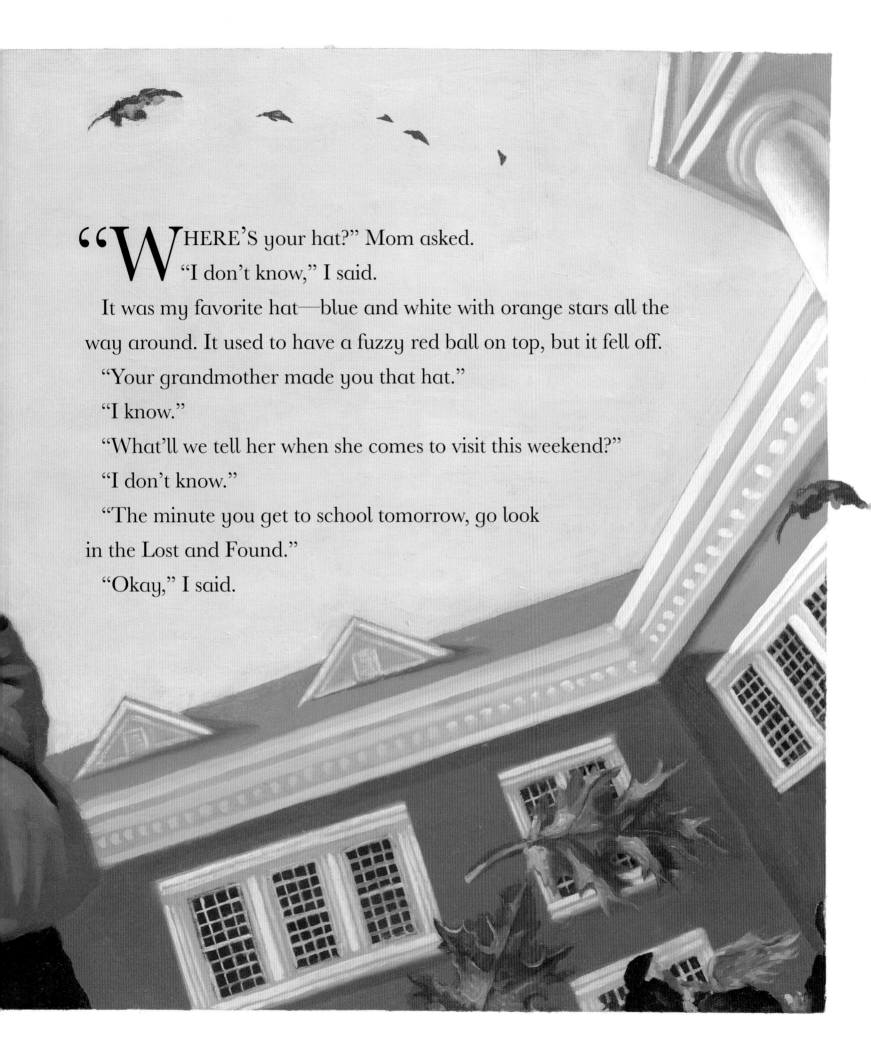

"WHERE'S your hat?" Mom asked.

"I don't know," I said.

It was my favorite hat—blue and white with orange stars all the way around. It used to have a fuzzy red ball on top, but it fell off.

"Your grandmother made you that hat."

"I know."

"What'll we tell her when she comes to visit this weekend?"

"I don't know."

"The minute you get to school tomorrow, go look in the Lost and Found."

"Okay," I said.

But the next morning I didn't go to the Lost and Found. I decided to find the hat myself. At recess, I looked by the basketball hoop and under the slide and behind the baseball backstop.

I asked Devaun if he had seen it. "It's blue and white with orange stars all the way around," I told him.

"Nope," he said. "Did you look in the Lost and Found?"

I made a face.

"I know," Devaun said. "I lost my baseball jacket last month, but I was too afraid to go see Mr. Rumkowsky."

"Can't you just get another hat?" asked Jessica.

I shook my head. "Gran made that one for me, and I have to find it—even if it means asking Mr. Rumkowsky."

"Uh-oh," they said.

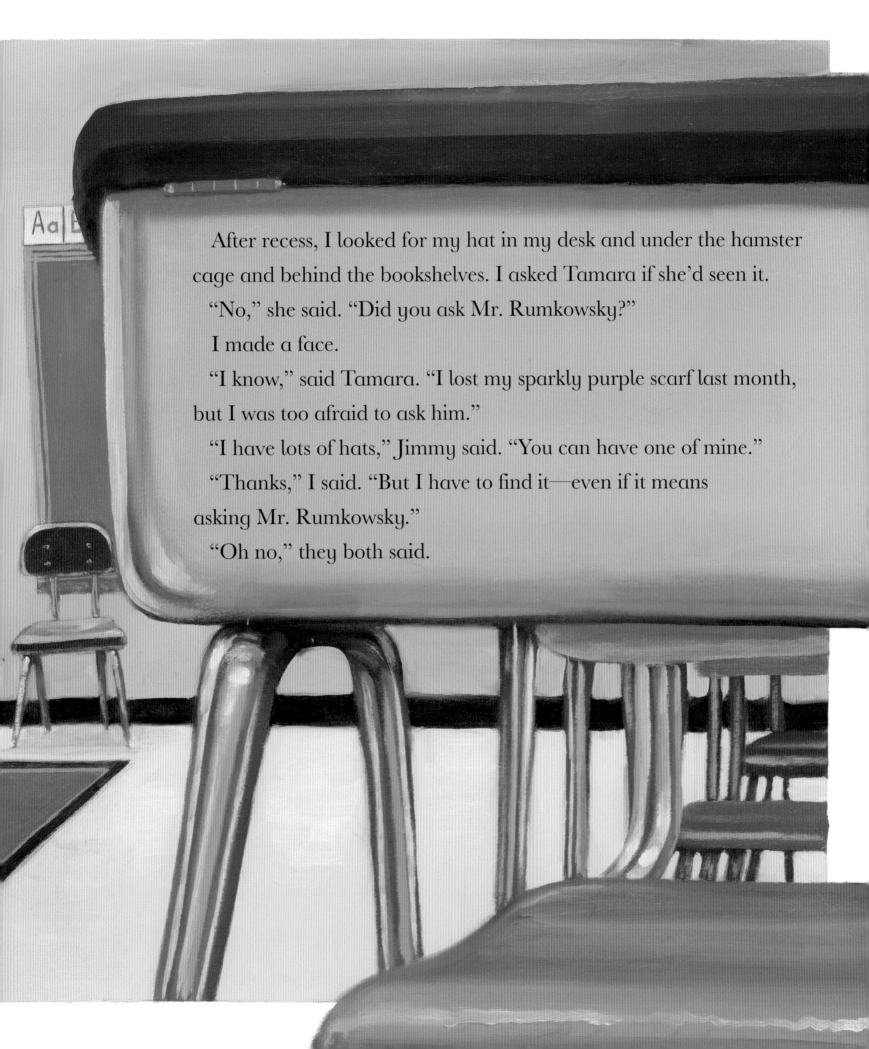

After recess, I looked for my hat in my desk and under the hamster cage and behind the bookshelves. I asked Tamara if she'd seen it.

"No," she said. "Did you ask Mr. Rumkowsky?"

I made a face.

"I know," said Tamara. "I lost my sparkly purple scarf last month, but I was too afraid to ask him."

"I have lots of hats," Jimmy said. "You can have one of mine."

"Thanks," I said. "But I have to find it—even if it means asking Mr. Rumkowsky."

"Oh no," they both said.

The next day my friends asked me if I'd found my hat. "No," I said. "I've looked everywhere. There's only one thing left to do—go to the Lost and Found."

"But that means talking to Mr. Rumkowsky," said Jimmy.

"Uh-oh," said the others.

"I know," I gulped. "He's really old. He's so old he was the custodian when my mom went to this school."

"Yeah," said Jessica. "He's always frowning and grumbling. And his office is way down at the end of that scary hallway behind the cafeteria."

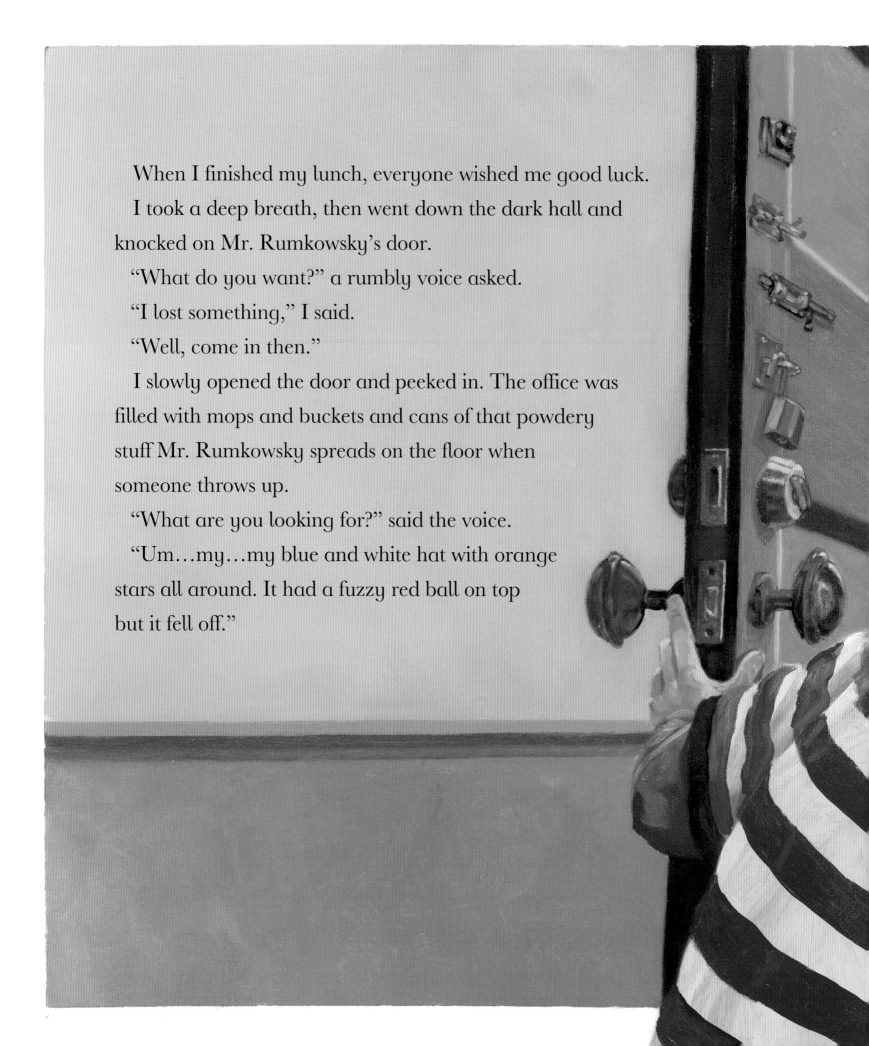

When I finished my lunch, everyone wished me good luck.

I took a deep breath, then went down the dark hall and knocked on Mr. Rumkowsky's door.

"What do you want?" a rumbly voice asked.

"I lost something," I said.

"Well, come in then."

I slowly opened the door and peeked in. The office was filled with mops and buckets and cans of that powdery stuff Mr. Rumkowsky spreads on the floor when someone throws up.

"What are you looking for?" said the voice.

"Um…my…my blue and white hat with orange stars all around. It had a fuzzy red ball on top but it fell off."

"What's so important about it?" he growled.

"It…um, I mean my grandmother made it," I said.

Mr. Rumkowsky scratched his head. "I think
I remember seeing a hat like that. Follow me."

That's when I saw the enormous box.

"I'll get the ladder," he said.

I peered down into the box and picked through the things on top. I didn't see my hat. But I saw Devaun's baseball jacket. And Tamara's sparkly purple scarf. When lunch period was over, I grabbed the jacket and the scarf and climbed back down the ladder.

"I didn't find it," I told Mr. Rumkowsky. "But I'll take these things to my friends."

"Come back sometime and look again," he said.

Devaun was happy to
get his jacket back.

Tamara put on her scarf and twirled around.

Jimmy, Jessica, and a kid I didn't even know asked me to look
for something the next time I went to Mr. Rumkowsky's office.

"Did you find your hat?"
Mom asked after supper.

"Not yet," I said.

"You must learn to take better
care of your things, Justin.
You're having to spend
an awful lot of time
looking for your hat."

I didn't say anything. I knew that already.

The next day I went back to Mr. Rumkowsky.

He dragged the ladder out again and I climbed into the box. I dug down deeper and found all sorts of weird stuff. But no hat.

"You can have those things you pulled out," said Mr. Rumkowsky. "Nobody wants them now."

"Thanks," I said. "See you tomorrow."

My friends went crazy over all the stuff I'd found.

I went back and looked through more
stuff. The things I found were getting
weirder and weirder.
But still no hat.

On Friday my mom dropped me off at school early.
"This afternoon when I pick you up, I'll have your
grandmother with me."

I didn't say anything. I knew that already.

I went straight to Mr. Rumkowsky's office.
"Keep digging," he said. It seemed like he wanted me
to find the hat as much as I did.

But I was about ready to give up. Everything I was
finding now was really old.

Finally I got to the bottom of the box.

"Do you see it?" Mr. Rumkowsky called down.

"It's not here," I said. "Just this dumb old pink sweater."

"Hmmm," he said. "Try looking under it."

I lifted it up.

"My hat!" I yelled. "Blue and white, with orange stars all the way around."

Mr. Rumkowsky helped me out of the box. "Are you sure it's yours?"

"It's mine, all right," I said. Then I noticed that it had a fuzzy red ball on top—just like the one that had fallen off my hat.

I turned it inside out. The tag said "Sally."

"Wait—that's my mom's name!" I said. "This must have been her hat when she was a kid!"

Mr. Rumkowsky actually smiled. "Come back anytime," he said.

I put the hat on and went to class. I wore it all day.

When Mom picked me up, my grandmother gave me a big hug. "I see you're wearing your hat," she said.

"Yes." I hugged her back.

"I made your mother a hat exactly like that when she was a little girl," Gran told me.

"I know," I said. My mom had a funny look on her face. I grinned but didn't say anything.

Gran looked at my mom, then at me. "I wonder what ever happened to the hat I made for your mother."

"Maybe you should ask Mr. Rumkowsky," I said.

"Rumkowsky?" Gran said. "Is he still at this school? Your mother was always afraid of him, but he's really a nice man."

I nodded.

I knew that already.

To the students, teachers, and staff at the
Paul Cuffee School in Providence, RI,
where I lose my hat all the time

—*B. H.*

For my parents

—*A. G.*

Ω

Published by
PEACHTREE PUBLISHERS
1700 Chattahoochee Avenue
Atlanta, Georgia 30318-2112
www.peachtree-online.com

Text © 2012 by Bill Harley
Illustrations © 2012 by Adam Gustavson

Art direction by Loraine M. Joyner

Illustrations were rendered in oil on prepared 100% cotton archival watercolor
paper; title is based on GautFonts's CornFed by J.F.Y. Daniel Gauthier;
text is typeset in Baskerville Infant.

Printed in September 2013 by Tien Wah in Malaysia
10 9 8 7 6 5 4 3

Library of Congress Cataloging-in-Publication Data

Harley, Bill, 1954-
 Lost and Found / written by Bill Harley ;
illustrated by Adam Gustavson.
  p. cm.
  Summary: Justin has lost the hat his grandmother made for him,
and if he is to find it in time for her visit he will have to go talk to
Mr. Rumkowsky, the gruff old school custodian in charge of the
Lost and Found.
  ISBN 13: 978-1-56145-628-4, ISBN 10: 1-56145-628-4
  [1. Lost and found possessions--Fiction. 2. Janitors--Fiction.
  3. Schools--Fiction.] I. Gustavson, Adam, ill. II. Title.
  PZ7.H22655Los 2012
  [E]--dc23
                                    2011020972